Quincy Rumpel
and the
Mystifying Experience

Quincy Rumpel
and the
Mystifying Experience

Betty Waterton

A Groundwood Book
Douglas & McIntyre
Toronto/Vancouver/Buffalo

Canadian Cataloguing in Publication Data

Waterton, Betty
   Quincy Rumpel and the mystifying experience

ISBN 0-88899-199-1

I. Title.

PS8595.A796Q5 1994   jC813'.54   C93-095544-7
PZ7.W3Qu 1994

Groundwood Books/Douglas & McIntyre Ltd.
585 Bloor Street West
Toronto, Ontario M6G 1K5

The publisher gratefully acknowledges the assistance of
the Ontario Arts Council and the Canada Council.

Design by Michael Solomon
Cover illustration by Eric Beddows
Printed and bound in Canada

For Madeleine, Jessica,
Daniel and Claire

CONTENTS

1
Mysterious Mail

Quincy clumped into the kitchen in her new western boots, sniffing her hands happily. "M'mmmm ... I just love that horsey smell! Smell my hands, Mom."

"Not now," said her mother. "We've got a letter."

The big brown envelope was addressed in large flowing handwriting to

The Rumpels
Rumpel Ranch
Cranberry Corners, B.C.

There was a tiny postal code squeezed into the corner.

"This has got to be from Aunt Fan in Toronto," said Mrs. Rumpel. "She hates postal codes."

She opened the envelope and, to the amazement of the five Rumpels, out tumbled a cascade of maps, folders and brochures.

"Why is she sending all this stuff to us?" wondered Mrs. Rumpel, picking up one of the pamphlets. "What do we want with a map of Toronto? And all these things about Niagara Falls, for Petey's sake ..."

"There must be a letter in there somewhere," said Mr. Rumpel.

"I can't find one. She must have forgotten to put it in."

"Listen to this, Mom." Leah, the middle Rumpel, flapped a paper in her mother's face. *"Niagara Falls, where romance begins . . .* could we please go there?"

"Hey," cried Morris. "Here's a whole bunch of coupons for Niagara Falls, and one of them is for a horrifying experience in a Haunted House! It says ghouls and monsters roam the passageways. Wow. I've never seen a ghoul in my whole entire life."

Quincy made a face at her little brother. "I'm sure there are a lot more elegant things to do at Niagara Falls than that." She picked up one of the pamphlets and began reading. "For instance, here's a fantastic boat ride 'through crashing waters surrounded by massive rock formations that have tamed the raging rapids for millions of years.' Now *that's* impressive. Oh, and do you know how the boat got its name? Well, just listen to this—"

"I'm sorry," interrupted Mrs. Rumpel. "But we don't have any plans to go back East. And I just can't imagine why Aunt Fan is sending all these things to us."

"Maybe she's got a job in the tourist bureau," said Leah, "and she's giving out free samples."

"Maybe she thinks you should take me on a trip to have a horrifying experience for my birthday," said Morris. "It's getting close—only seven months away."

"Well, there's one way to find out what this is all about," said Mr. Rumpel. "We'll just have to phone Aunt Fan."

"Do it, Mom," coaxed Leah. "Phone her now."

"I will. After six." Mrs. Rumpel's voice was firm. "I must say, this is the strangest mail we've ever had from Aunt Fan."

"Mystifying mail, I would call it," said Quincy. "What's for supper?"

2
An Invitation

After supper, Quincy was leading her horse, Roxy, into the barn when Leah came running out of the house, her blonde hair flying and her arms waving like windmills.

"Guess what, Quincy," she gasped, skidding to a stop in the sawdust. "Mom phoned Aunt Fan just now and do you know why she sent us all those things? I'll bet you could never guess in a million years. It's absolutely incredible. I never thought it would actually happen. Of course, it's not to say we'll actually get there, but we might. I think. Wouldn't you just *love* to sleep in one of those heart-shaped beds at Niagara Falls?"

"Leah, you're talking gibberish. What are you trying to tell me?"

"Aunt Fan thinks we should go down to Toronto and surprise her so that was why she sent all those things to us, only she forgot to put the letter in the envelope . . ."

"How can we surprise Aunt Fan?"

"Not her, silly. Grams. Our great-grandmother. For a surprise for her ninety-first birthday. Mom and Dad are talking it over right this minute, and *maybe we'll go!*"

"Grams is going to be ninety-one? Wow. Oh, I'd love to go and surprise her. I can remember her a little bit, but I don't suppose you can. You were too young. She used to give us humbugs."

Leah frowned in concentration. "I think I can remember humbugs."

Quincy slipped the halter off her buckskin mare, then put an armful of hay in the horse's stall.

She planted a kiss on the velvet nose. "There you go, sweetie." Then she closed the bottom half of the barn door and ran into the house after her sister.

Mr. Rumpel was on the phone.

Mrs. Rumpel was sitting at the table, making a list.

Leah was riffling through pamphlets.

Morris was studying a map of Canada, while strawberry jam dripped onto it from his toast.

As the screen door banged shut behind her, Quincy asked breathlessly, "Are we going?"

Mrs. Rumpel looked up and put her finger to her lips. "Shhhhh . . . your father is on the phone to the travel agent now. If we're able to get a seat sale on the airlines, we might go."

"By air? Really? Do you mean it?"

Her mother nodded.

As Mr. Rumpel hung up the phone, his family searched his face for a clue.

He looks kind of worried, thought Quincy. *I guess that means we didn't get a seat sale. Poor Grams, now she'll never get to see me in my woolly chaps . . .*

We're not going. I just know it. Sighing dramatically, Leah put away the brochure showing a heart-shaped bed with a furry bedspread.

Morris shoved the rest of his toast into his mouth, then scraped the jam off the map of the Great Lakes and ate it. *Oh, well, at least now I won't have to put Leonardo and Donatello into a boarding kennel.*

Mrs. Rumpel studied her husband's face. *I know that look,* she thought. *We're definitely not going.*

They were all wrong.

3

Plans

It turned out that Mr. Rumpel's worried look was because the airline did indeed have a seat sale on, and so he had made reservations. Now all he had to worry about was paying for the tickets.

"Oh, but it will be so wonderful to surprise Grams on her birthday," said Mrs. Rumpel. "I know it will cost a lot, but she's the only grandmother I've got left."

"And she's our only *great*-grandmother," added Quincy.

"I don't know if I can remember her or not," said Leah. "But I'd sure like to see Niagara Falls. Is it very far from Toronto?"

"Look on the map," Morris told her. "Sort of under the jam mark. I think I'll just take Leonardo and Donatello with me. It will be cheaper than boarding them out while we're away."

"Don't be silly," said his mother. "You're not taking those goldfish to Ontario. The McAddams children will probably be glad to look after them for you. And, Leah, I'm not at all sure we'll be able to get to Niagara Falls."

Suddenly Quincy thought of her new horse. "Oh, poor Roxy! She's just getting used to being here and now I'm going to leave her. I guess I'll have to take her over to the McAddamses, too. I hope she won't be too distraught."

"What about Snowflake? And Fireweed? And the chickens?" asked Leah.

"I'll speak to Mrs. McAddams about all this," said Mrs. Rumpel. "I'm sure we can work something out —especially if we pay Poppy and Muggsy and Crocus to look after them."

"Crocus?" cried Morris. "I'm not paying Crocus to look after my little guys. She's only three years old. She'd probably squeeze them or something."

"Morris, stop worrying about your dumb fish," groaned Quincy.

"Well, I know what I'm going to do when I get home," grumbled Morris. "I'm going into the gold-fish-boarding business. If Crocus can earn money doing it, I sure can. There must be lots of people who want to leave their pet fish somewhere when they go away."

"Enough about goldfish," said Mrs. Rumpel. "We have other things to think about. I want you girls to sort the clothes you're taking. Aunt Fan thinks it would be nice to have the surprise party at her summer cottage at Lake Wannabanana, so you'll need mostly just camp clothes."

"Do we land near there?" Leah wanted to know.

16

"No, we land at Pearson Airport. We'll rent a car from there," said Mr. Rumpel.

"A Rent-A-Wreck!" cried Morris.

"A white stretch limo!" cried Leah.

"What about a 4-wheel-drive Jeep?" asked Quincy. "They're good for the bush."

"Lake Wannabanana isn't exactly in the bush," said her mother.

"We're getting a mini-van," said Mr. Rumpel. "It's all arranged."

"A mini-van would be good," said Morris, Leah and Quincy.

4

A Shopping Spree

The next day, preparations began in earnest, with a shopping spree to the mall in Cranberry Corners by Mrs. Rumpel and the girls.

At the end of the exhausting day, Leah went home with a red bathing suit (with a double-ruffle waist) and some pink plastic beach sandals.

Quincy, after much deliberation, purchased a sequined baseball cap and flowered overalls.

Mrs. Rumpel bought socks for her husband and Morris, some one-size-fits-all jeans for herself, and new underwear for everybody.

They were halfway home when Quincy exclaimed, "Grams! What are we going to get Grams for her birthday?"

"Oh, dear," gasped Mrs. Rumpel, taking her foot off the accelerator. "I'd forgotten all about a birthday present. I wonder what we can get her?"

"I could knit her some bed socks," said Leah. "If I had a little more time. It takes three months for each sock."

"I've got a nice picture of Roxy and me," said Quincy. "I'm in my woolly chaps . . . why are you slowing down the car, Mom?"

"Because I'm thinking. Actually, a picture may not be a bad idea. I mean one of the whole family . . ."

"I'll wear my new bathing suit," said Leah.

"We'll have a nice one taken at the Cranberry Corners Portrait Studio," went on Mrs. Rumpel. "After I get my hair done."

This decided, the car spurted forward down the dusty road to Rumpel Ranch.

***

But Mrs. Rumpel had reckoned without Mr. Rumpel.

"I am not going into town to have my picture taken," he said. "I'm far too busy picking bugs off the apple trees." And that was that.

In the end, because time was running out, their neighbour, Dr. McAddams, came over and took a Polaroid snapshot of the Rumpels standing in front of their house.

Though Quincy's horse was hanging her head over Mrs. Rumpel's shoulder—obliterating her new hairdo, and several chickens managed to get in the picture, at least everyone was smiling.

"Grams will love it," pronounced Quincy. "It's *so* good of Roxy."

That afternoon, Grandpa's old horse Fireweed, Quincy's new horse Roxy, Snowflake the dog, Morris's goldfish and all the chickens were moved to the McAddamses nearby ranch for safekeeping.

The next morning the five Rumpels piled into the car with their suitcases, backpacks, tote-bags and a bouquet of sweet peas. As they headed down the road towards the Cranberry Corners airport, the sun, all pink and gold, was just coming up.

5

On the Way

As they straggled into the empty waiting room, Mrs. Rumpel said, "I knew it. I just knew we'd be the first ones here."

"We're always the first ones everywhere," grumbled Quincy. "Dad never gives us time to get ready, even. Look at Morris — he still has his pyjama top on, for Pete's sake."

"And my hair," moaned Leah. "I didn't have time to do it this morning and it's a mess."

Quincy looked at her sister's tousled mane. "It sort of is, isn't it? Come on into the washroom and I'll fix it."

She was still working on Leah's hair when the boarding announcement came.

"It's worse than before!" wailed Leah, inspecting her dripping wet hairdo. "I can't go on the plane looking like this!"

Grabbing some paper towels, Quincy began blotting her sister's head.

"The plane's going! The plane's going!" yelled Mrs. Rumpel, bursting into the washroom.

And so it was, that while the Rumpels were the first passengers to arrive at the airport, they were the last to board the aircraft.

***

Once aboard the twin-engine plane that would take them to the big airport in Vancouver, Mr. and Mrs. Rumpel stowed their hand luggage in the overhead compartment, fastened their seatbelts and settled back with sighs of relief.

Leah and Quincy, who declined to part with their backpacks, endured the flight with them under their feet.

"It's kind of uncomfortable," whispered Leah, as she settled into the window seat. "But at least nobody will steal them. Look at that man over there . . . do you think he might be a hijacker?"

"Don't be silly." Quincy snapped on her seatbelt. "I've seen him in the pet store in town. He raises lop-eared rabbits."

She had just got her long legs arranged onto her backpack and was surreptitiously looking around for suspicious-looking characters when Leah poked her in the ribs. "Can I ask a tiny favour, Quince? A favour-ette? Do you mind changing seats? I think I'd feel safer if I couldn't see out."

"What are they doing?" asked Mr. Rumpel, looking up the aisle to where Leah and Quincy appeared to be engaged in mortal combat.

"I'm not sure. I think they're changing seats. Now they're switching backpacks . . ."

At that moment a shrill voice behind them piped up, "We're going to my great-grandma's ninety-first birthday party. That's pretty old. My parents are pretty old, too. That's them sitting right ahead of us. My mom is thirty-seven and my dad is forty-three. He's starting to get bald but he still has hair on his chest. I don't have any hair on mine yet. My mom tried to lose ten pounds last week, but she couldn't do it so she had to buy one-size-fits-all jeans instead of the regular kind. Those are my sisters sitting up there. Quincy is the one with her head sticking up. She has red hair, but you can't see it because of her new baseball cap. It cost $7.98 plus tax. She hasn't got a boyfriend but she almost had one. His name was Freddie. Quincy had a pimple once. Sometimes my sister Leah throws up. She's the one with a scarf on her head. She's never been in a plane before. But I have. I went to visit Grandma and Grandpa Rumpel all by myself— "

Just then the engines revved up. For a minute or two Morris tried to shout above their noise, but eventually he gave up. Leaning forward, he pressed his nose against the window and, to the relief of all those seated near him, fell silent.

***

The Rumpels' stopover to change planes at Vancouver proved to be a brief one.

23

Followed by the rest of the family, Mr. Rumpel charged through the terminal, crying, "Gate 28! Where's Gate 28?"

"We'd better all join hands so we don't get separated," gasped Mrs. Rumpel, grabbing the back of Morris's jacket.

"Ma!" Protesting loudly, Morris wriggled out of her grasp.

"I think I see a washroom," said Quincy. "I'll catch up with you guys later . . ."

"No, you won't," said her mother. "You stay right with us."

"My sandal's coming off," cried Leah. "Don't go so fast."

Suddenly Mr. Rumpel came to an abrupt halt. Crashing into him went Mrs. Rumpel, clutching her purse, tote-bag, raincoat, umbrella, travel slippers and the rapidly wilting bouquet. Quincy, Leah and Morris skidded in behind her.

"We have to go back," announced Mr. Rumpel, unhooking a sweet pea from his sweater. "We've been going the wrong way. Step on it, everybody!"

"I'm hungry," whined Morris, as they turned around and began surging back against the oncoming tide of passengers. "I need food."

"I need a washroom," muttered Quincy.

"I need my other shoes," said Leah. "Can we please stop and let me put on my other shoes?"

"No food. No washroom. No other shoes," said Mr. Rumpel grimly. "We have another plane to catch."

6

Tight Quarters

"Wow!" gasped Morris, as the Rumpels filed onto their new aircraft. "This is *one big plane*!"

As soon as they were seated, Mrs. Rumpel handed out travel slippers to her family. "It's best not to have on tight shoes when you're flying such a long way," she told them.

"Mother!" hissed Quincy. "Nobody else is putting on slippers, and I'm sure not going to."

"Me, neither," said Leah. "Anyway, my sandals are too loose as it is."

As Mr. Rumpel and Morris also waved their slippers away, Mrs. Rumpel jammed them all back in her bag —except for her own, which she put on.

"This is *so neat*, Quincy," said Leah, when the lights dimmed and the in-flight movie started. "I didn't know they'd have a movie on the plane."

"And it's *The Black Stallion*, my very favourite! But maybe I'd better go to the washroom while it's dark and nobody can see me. Are you coming?"

But Leah was already engrossed in the picture. Squeezing past her, Quincy hunched down and crept along the aisle towards the back of the darkened plane.

It was some time later that Leah realized her sister hadn't returned. Leaning forward, she tapped her mother on the shoulder.

"Quincy hasn't come back from the washroom."

"Oh, good grief," cried Mrs. Rumpel.

Mr. Rumpel, who had been dozing beside her, woke up with a start. "What? What's the matter?"

"It's Quincy. She hasn't come back from the washroom!"

As Mrs. Rumpel struggled out of her seatbelt, a stewardess hurried towards her. "Is something the matter?"

"Quincy's stuck in the bathroom," replied Morris. "But she'll be okay. Don't stop the movie."

The stewardess raced down the aisle, followed by Mrs. Rumpel, Mr. Rumpel, another flight attendant pushing a cart of drinks, and a little group of helpful passengers.

Banging noises were coming from behind a washroom door at the back. These were followed by a voice muttering, "Oh, darn, darn, *darn*!"

"Quincy? Is that you?" cried Mrs. Rumpel. "What's the matter, dear? Are you locked in?"

From behind the door came a loud, resigned sigh, then the sound of a bolt sliding.

The door slowly opened and out squeezed Quincy,

in her flowered overalls. She looked hot and flustered, and her straps were done up wrong.

"You wouldn't believe how *small* it is in there," she told Leah later. "It's positively the *very last* time I wear overalls on a plane."

7

A Tale of Moonstones

Clutching their belongings, the five Rumpels were swept along in the throng of disembarking passengers at Toronto's Pearson Airport.

"Stay together. Stay together!" Mrs. Rumpel urged her family.

"Man!" exclaimed Morris, who was bringing up the rear. "And we thought the Vancouver one was big! Hey, Leah, see those people riding in that little train thing? They must be really important." And he hopped respectfully out of the way.

"Oh, yes! Just look at that person at the very front — the one with the briefcase. Do you suppose that's the prime minister?"

But Morris didn't know.

Eventually the Rumpels found their way to the luggage carousel, where they joined the waiting crowd.

This is exciting, thought Quincy, gazing around. *Here we are brushing shoulders with the rest of the world. We don't know who anyone is . . . and nobody knows who we are. For all they know I could be a Russian exchange student . . . or a Greenpeace worker, back from a whale-watching expedition in the Arctic . . .*

Her thoughts were interrupted by Leah, who suddenly cried, "A beagle! I just saw a beagle in a little green jacket."

"Where? Where?" Morris swivelled his head around. "Oh, I see it. It's on a leash. It's probably a police sniffer dog. You know, to sniff for bombs . . . "

"Morris, it says *Agriculture Canada* on his jacket," said Quincy. "I think they sniff for sausages and stuff."

"But they *could* sniff for bombs. Like maybe a sausage bomb . . . "

Just then there was a murmur from the crowd — "Here they come . . ." — as luggage began rolling past on the carousel.

Mrs. Rumpel, who had tied coloured tassels to all their suitcases before they left home, cried, "Watch for our yellow pom-poms."

***

At last the Rumpels found themselves, together with all their belongings, in their rented red mini-van on the way to Aunt Fan's cottage.

"Your great-grandmother is going to be so thrilled to see you children," said Mrs. Rumpel as they drove along. "Leah was just a baby when she saw you last, and Morris wasn't even born."

"I remember her, though," said Quincy. "She let me polish all her little souvenir spoons. And she had beautiful long silver hair in a swirl on top of her head."

"And Mom said you got it all tangled up once, trying to braid it while you were eating maple syrup," said Leah.

"Grams didn't have an easy life, with Gramps away at sea so much," went on Mrs. Rumpel. "She practically raised Aunt Fan and the other nine children all by herself."

Leah nodded sympathetically. "Sort of like a single mom, I guess."

"Except that Gramps did get home occasionally. And he always brought presents — brass gongs and things like that. Once he brought Grams a gorgeous purple silk sari from India, woven with real gold thread."

"And she sold it to buy winter boots for her children," added Quincy, who knew the story well.

"And once he brought home a stuffed armadillo, and an umbrella stand made out of an elephant's foot," added Morris. "Do you suppose she's still got them? I wouldn't mind having a stuffed armadillo."

Leah groaned. "That is *so* gross. They're an endangered species, you know."

"Yes, and don't you ever breathe a word about that dead stuff being in our family, Morris Rumpel. It would be *so* embarrassing." Quincy glared at her brother.

"I doubt Grams still has those things," said Mrs. Rumpel. "She's living in a retirement home now."

"Mom, tell us again about the moonstones," coaxed Leah.

"Ah, yes, the moonstones . . ." Mrs. Rumpel's eyes had a faraway look. "Aunt Fan saw them once, and they were the most beautiful things she had ever seen. They were in a little black velvet bag, and they glowed like milky moonlight. It was said that Gramps brought them home because they reminded him of moonlight on the Arabian Sea."

Leah sighed. *". . . moonlight on the Arabian Sea.* Can't you just picture it?"

"I wonder what happened to them . . ." mused Quincy.

"Grams never would talk about them," said Mrs. Rumpel. "In fact, she was downright cagey about the moonstones *and* about Gramps, for that matter. She'd say, 'It's all in the past. *Let the dead past bury its dead.*'"

Leah shivered. "That's spooky."

"It's mystifying, all right," said Quincy. "And I intend to get to the bottom of it."

8

Lake Wannabanana

It was late in the afternoon when Mrs. Rumpel exclaimed, "Lake Wannabanana! Here's Lake Wannabanana, everybody! We're close to Aunt Fan's now. I think I remember this spot, even, although the trees seem bigger. Now, watch for a brown cottage. And she always had an old painted milk can by the door, full of nasturtiums."

After a few minutes of driving around, Quincy said, "There are hundreds of brown cottages with milk cans, Mom."

"There do seem to be a lot more than there used to be," admitted her mother, as they lurched down one maple-shaded lane after another. "Just look for her name."

"I'm hungry," whined Morris.

"I'm thirsty, and Morris's feet are making me sick, and this window doesn't open," gasped Leah.

"It's so hot, and I'm getting bug-eyed from looking so hard. All I want to do is go swimming in that lake." Quincy pointed to the sparkling blue water. "I feel like jumping in right this minute."

Morris began to peel off his T-shirt. "Me, too."

"It does look inviting," admitted Mrs. Rumpel.

"Now, hold your horses, everybody," said Mr. Rumpel. "We must be getting close. I'm going to try this road . . ."

"We've been down here twice already, Harvey." Mrs. Rumpel's voice sounded weary. "This is the third time we've passed that weird purple place with the statues of that little girl and all those gnomes."

"Mom, that's Snow White and the seven dwarfs," said Leah.

"There . . ." Mrs. Rumpel pointed to a brown cottage on the other side of the road, half-hidden in the trees. Beside the door was a blue milk can filled with nasturtiums.

"That's it. I'm sure that's it. I think I remember those curtains . . ."

The red mini-van slowed to a stop, and the five Rumpels swarmed out and up to the door of the cottage.

"Yoo-hoo!" called Mrs. Rumpel, opening it. "We're here!"

No answer.

"I'll bet everybody's at the lake," said Quincy. "Let's put on our bathing suits and go down and surprise them."

This seemed like a good idea to the others. Retrieving their bathing suits from their luggage, they trooped into the cottage and dispersed.

33

"Now, this is what I call a *real* bathroom." Quincy's voice rang out from down the hall. "There's even a jacuzzi in here."

"Aunt Fan has a waterbed!" called out Leah from a bedroom.

"Auntie has got some nice new furniture." From another bedroom, Mrs. Rumpel's voice came in short gasps as she struggled into her multicolour Spandex bathing suit with tummy control panel.

"And she's got some mighty fine food in the fridge!" Mr. Rumpel shouted gleefully from the kitchen.

"I FOUND A HOT-TUB," screeched Morris from somewhere. "Come and see it, everybody!"

Following his shrieks, the others surged through the cottage. With cries of delight, the five Rumpels leaped into the cedar-lined hot-tub.

Now, thought Quincy, as she sat blissfully submerged up to her chin in the bubbling water, *if only Dad doesn't start singing . . .*

But he did.

"Day-oh . . . da-a-ay-oh! Daylight come and me *no* wanna go home . . ." sang Mr. Rumpel lustily.

Suddenly a voice from behind them quavered, "All right, everybody, FREEZE!"

The Rumpels turned and saw two figures standing behind them, clutching tennis racquets. They were wearing spotless white shorts and shirts and had green sweaters tied over their shoulders.

34

"Ha, ha," chortled Morris. "You guys just said 'freeze,' and we're sitting in a *hot*-tub!"

"Hi," smiled Mrs. Rumpel, yanking off her bathing cap and fluffing out her hair. "We're the Rumpels. We just got in from Cranberry Corners. Who are you folks?"

The lady tennis player cleared her throat. "This is Bill, and I'm Hillary. . . . What are you people doing here?"

"We're freshening up," Quincy told her. "That was some trip, believe you me."

"Man, were we sweating!" added Morris.

"We're here for Great-grandma Twistle's birthday," said Leah. "But I hope we can get to Niagara Falls, too, because I'd really love to sleep in a heart-shaped bed. They don't have any of those in Cranberry Corners, you know — "

"Hey, this is like, cool, man," interrupted Morris. "You ought to try it." Holding his nose, he disappeared under the swirling water.

As Morris's green rubber flippers fluttered briefly in the air, Bill said, "Oh, so you must be Miss Twistle's relatives?"

"Of course," said Mrs. Rumpel. "Aren't you?"

Bill and Hillary shook their heads. "We're her neighbours, though. Miss Twistle lives over there . . ." Hillary pointed her racquet across the road.

"The purple house? With the purple milk can?" gasped Mrs. Rumpel, scrambling out of the hot-tub. "But I was so sure Auntie's house was brown . . . "

35

"It was," said Hillary as the Rumpels scurried around gathering up their belongings. "Until last year, when she won the raffle at the hardware store."

"It was paint," said Bill. "She won twenty-five cans of purple paint."

9

A Cryptic Note

Their feet squishing in their hastily donned shoes, the five Rumpels slunk away across the narrow dirt road.

"I'm afraid there's nobody here." Mr. Rumpel peered at the purple cottage. "There's no car, and all the windows are closed."

As they went up the winding path, the seven dwarfs watched them stonily, and Snow White smiled her frozen smile.

"Auntie never used to have those," said Mrs. Rumpel. "It's no wonder I didn't recognize the place."

"I guess she won them at a raffle, too," said Leah.

The door of the cottage was locked. There was no note, and except for a faded purple bathing suit dangling from the clothesline, no sign of life anywhere.

"It's strange she didn't leave us a key," said Mrs. Rumpel, lifting up the doormat and looking underneath. "I wonder . . . Quincy, what are you doing rooting around in the nasturtiums?"

"Looking for a note. If she didn't leave a key, she must have left a note."

"Wouldn't it be on the door?" asked Leah.

"Not necessarily. Suppose she didn't want anybody else to read it. Now, if we were Aunt Fan, where would we leave it, h'mmm?"

"Under the dwarfs!" cried Morris instantly. "I'll start with Grumpy . . ."

The other Rumpels gazed around thoughtfully. Suddenly Quincy snapped her fingers.

"Aha!" she said, striding over to the clothesline. "There's something strange about that bathing suit. Why would Aunt Fan hang it up by just one clothespin? This is very mystifying indeed."

"Maybe the other one pranged off," suggested Leah.

"Where is it, then? It's not on the grass." Quincy reached into the clothespin bag. There was the sound of scrabbling, then — "Ta-da!" And she pulled out a folded card.

"That's a Christmas card!" exclaimed Leah. "It's got a Santa Claus on it."

"Yes, but look on the back. It's our note!"

"That woman certainly does believe in recycling," said Mr. Rumpel.

Reaching out for the card, Mrs. Rumpel held it at arm's length. "I can't make head nor tail out of this. Are you sure it's for us?"

"Yes, I'm sure, Mom." Quincy took the card. "See, it starts off with R's. That must stand for Rumpels. But the rest of it is rather an enigma, I must say."

As they hung over Quincy's shoulder, the others studied the message:

R's, red but. al. re G, rtn. YYZ ASAP! AF.

"A cryptic note!" cried Leah.

"Very mystifying," admitted Quincy.

Eventually, however, the note was deciphered. Or almost.

Rumpels, red button alert re Grams, return YYZ as soon as possible! Aunt Fan.

"But what's YYZ?" wondered the Rumpels.

"Come on, everybody," cried Mrs. Rumpel, rushing over to the car. "We'd better hurry!"

"Where to?" said Leah. "How can we go when we don't know where YYZ is, Mom?"

But when Morris took out his suitcase to look for his secret stash of chocolate bars, the puzzle was solved. There on the baggage ticket in large letters was their destination — YYZ. Toronto.

10
Red Button Alert

S till in their bathing suits, and sitting on their tow-els, the Rumpels sped back towards the city.

"Red button alert. I wonder what that means." Mrs. Rumpel's voice was shaky.

Mr. Rumpel patted her knee. "Ninety-one is a good old age, Rose. You have to be prepared for almost anything."

"I know," sniffled Mrs. Rumpel.

"Ninety-one isn't so old if you're a Galapagos turtle," said Morris cheerfully.

"Maybe it's something good about Grams," said Leah. "Like maybe she won the lottery or something, or maybe she's getting married. That would be nice."

"Don't be dumb, Leah. Red button alert is definitely *not* something nice," scoffed Quincy. *My great-grand-mother is ninety-one years old,* she thought. *I can't even imagine being that old. But then, I can't imagine being thirty-one. I guess it doesn't matter much after that how old you are . . .*

For a while the trip continued in silence, with every-one lost in their own thoughts.

At last Mr. Rumpel said, "Watch for the skyline of Toronto, kids. We're getting close."

"The Hockey Hall of Fame. I wanna see the Hockey Hall of Fame." Morris pressed his nose against the window. "I heard they've got all this great new stuff, like a real team dressing room full of real old socks and everything . . ."

"I think I see the CN Tower," cried Leah. "Right over there . . ."

"That's a church," Quincy told her. "The CN Tower is higher than that. It's taller than the Empire State Building, even."

Mrs. Rumpel looked up at the dark clouds gathering overhead. "I think it's going to rain."

The next minute it did. As the weather closed in, the approaching skyline disappeared. In their red mini-van, the Rumpels groped their way through the down-pour, finally arriving some time later at Aunt Fan's condominium.

"So this is what they call Harbourfront." Peering through the rain, Mr. Rumpel climbed somewhat stiffly out of the van.

"It's bigger than the whole town of Cranberry Corners," marvelled Leah.

"Where's the Hockey Hall of Fame?" wondered Morris.

"How can you people be so crass?" asked Quincy. "We're here on a red button alert, you know."

"You're right, Quincy. Oh, Grams, Grams, we're coming!" cried Mrs. Rumpel, running up to the front door of the condominium. As she stood beside the intercom hunting for Aunt Fan's buzzer, the other Rumpels clustered around her, clutching their luggage and chattering excitedly.

They were still in their bathing suits.

11
Twistle Pickles

They rode up in the elevator with three ladies dressed in crisp summer dresses, straw hats and gloves.

"If you're wondering why we're in our bathing suits," said Quincy. "It's because of the red button alert."

"We came all the way from Cranberry Corners today," Morris told them. "And, man, are we getting tired."

"You see," added Leah, "we were in Bill and Hillary's hot-tub but we didn't know it was. Theirs, I mean. We thought it was Aunt Fan's, but Aunt Fan's was really the purple cottage. Well, you could have knocked us over with a feather . . ."

"Perhaps you know my aunt, Fantasia Twistle, on the sixteenth floor?" asked Mrs. Rumpel. The three ladies shook their heads. "We came for Gram's ninety-first birthday," she went on. "It's supposed to be a surprise, but now we're afraid something terrible has happened — because of the red button alert . . ."

Just then the elevator whispered to a stop. "Guess we'll have to leave you ladies now," said Mr. Rumpel. "It was nice meeting you. Be sure to look us up if you ever get to Cranberry Corners. We're the only Rumpels in the phone book."

With little waves and a "YO!" from Morris, the five Rumpels trooped off the elevator.

Just as they reached Aunt Fan's door, it was flung open. There stood Aunt Fan herself, in voluminous green shorts and a yellow sweatshirt that said *I* ♡ *Lake Wannabanana.* Her newly red hair, fastened on top of her head with combs, had come loose, and long strands of it flopped about her neck. For a moment she peered at the Rumpels nearsightedly. Then, hauling them inside, she shut the door quickly.

"Because of Prince Albert," she said, enfolding the Rumpels one by one in a warm, bony hug.

Prince Albert? Quincy's blue eyes glanced expertly about the room, but there was just a gangly dark-haired boy in jeans and Blue Jays T-shirt standing by the window.

"Prince Albert?" whispered Leah.

Quincy shrugged. "You never can tell, these days."

"What about Grams?" As Mrs. Rumpel choked out the words, she began to sniffle.

Aunt Fan handed her a white handkerchief. "Brace yourself for a shock, dear . . ."

A shock! I knew this had to be bad news, thought Quincy. *This is real life, and it's happening to you, Quincy Rumpel. Your very own great-grandmother—*

your link with your roots — is gone. And . . . Great-aunt Fan is an orphan.

". . . . gone," Aunt Fan was saying. "Since early this morning. And Mr. Panagopolous's family hasn't heard from him, either. Kip and I rushed back from the cottage as soon as I got the message . . ."

"Mr. Panagopolous?" Quincy stared at her.

"Her friend from the retirement home. Weren't you listening, child?"

"I knew it," cried Leah. "She *did* get married!"

"Of course they didn't get married. At least, I don't think they did . . ." Suddenly Aunt Fan looked doubtful.

Seemingly in a daze, Mrs. Rumpel wandered into the living room, where she collapsed onto the piano stool and began twirling slowly from side to side. "Do you think they were . . . *kidnapped*?"

"You're making a damp mark, Rose," said Aunt Fan. "Sit on your hankie. No, it seems they took off in Mr. P.'s old convertible — a yellow Mustang."

Whew! thought Quincy. *That's a relief. At least Aunt Fan isn't an orphan yet . . .*

"Kip," Aunt Fan was saying, "come and meet your cousins from B.C. Kip's staying with me for a few days while his folks are at the big pickle convention down in the States. They're in the pickle business."

"Twistle Pickles," said Kip. " 'More Crunch in Our Bunch.' I'm Rudyard Kipling Twistle."

H'mmm. He's taller than me, and older, I think. And sort of cute . . . Quincy's thoughts were interrupted by the sound of a giggle.

"Quincy thought you might be Prince Albert," tittered Leah. Quincy gave her a kick.

"*There* is Prince Albert, the monster." Aunt Fan pointed to the corner, where a blue and yellow parrot glared out from behind the chewed-up foliage of a potted palm tree.

"Well, I hope this friend of Grams is younger than she is," said Mr. Rumpel. "Driving around this town is not for the faint-hearted."

"Oh, he is. Mr. P. is not even ninety yet."

"Did . . . did she take a suitcase?" Mrs. Rumpel's voice quavered.

"Apparently not. Just her red purse, and her Medicare card."

"Maybe they went to Niagara Falls," said Leah. "That's where I'd like to spend my honeymoon."

Everyone stared at her.

"Me, too," said Morris. "In the Haunted House."

"Not me," said Quincy. "I'd want to do something more exciting—like go hot air ballooning. Like in that movie, *Around the World in Eighty Days*. Of course, they didn't go all the way around the world in the balloon, but that's what I'd like to do some day. I'd probably need a pretty big one — maybe you could come, too, Leah."

"Not me," protested her sister.

"I'll come," offered Morris.

"Enough about balloons," cried Mrs. Rumpel. "What about Grams?"

Just then a shrill beeping sounded somewhere in the apartment.

"Smoke alarm!" yelled Mr. Rumpel. Waving his towel, he loped towards the kitchen.

"My casserole!" yelled Aunt Fan, galloping after him.

12

Scalloped Potatoes

"Smoke alarm! Smoke alarm!" squawked another voice.

With a ruffling sound and a blur of blue and yellow feathers, Prince Albert swooped past the startled Rumpels and out of the room.

Luckily the casserole was only slightly charred, so while Aunt Fan made supper, the Rumpels finally changed out of their bathing suits.

"Except for that gross elephant foot in the front hall and the armadillo in the living room, this is a beautiful apartment, isn't it?" said Leah, as she and Quincy got dressed. "Did you see that white fireplace? I think it's real marble. And that crystal chandelier—just like in *Phantom of the Opera.*"

Quincy nodded. "It is *très* elegant. And those palm trees in every room are *très, très* exotic."

They wandered around the apartment, looking at souvenir plates of the royal family, old photographs and paintings that decorated the white walls.

"Look, Quince." Leah was gazing at an old photograph in a silver frame. It was of a young woman with laughing eyes. Her long fair hair was swooped up on top of her head, and she wore a high-necked, lace-trimmed white blouse.

"She's so pretty. And her hair looks naturally curly. She seems to be laughing at something. I wonder what it was . . ."

"That must be Grams," said Quincy. "She looks awfully young, doesn't she? That must have been before she had ten children."

"I think she looks sort of like me, don't you? Her hair seems blonde, too."

"Huh. It looks more red to me." Then Quincy pointed to the painted portrait of a bearded young man in a gold-braided uniform. He was smiling stiffly, showing two rows of gleaming white teeth. Perched on his shoulder was a large blue and yellow bird. The painting was signed *F. Twistle.*

"I bet that's our great-grandfather. And I'll bet that's Prince Albert, only he looks kind of stuffed. And Gramps looks as if he had false teeth."

"It's really hard to paint smiles," said Leah. "When I paint teeth they always come out looking like that, too."

"He was probably an admiral or something. Admiral Twistle . . ." Quincy's eyes shone with admiration. "I guess it's because of him that we all like the water so much."

Just then from the potted palm in the corner of the dining room came a screech, "Swab the decks, you dirty dogs . . ."

"Oh, do shut up, you bad bird," said Aunt Fan crossly, carrying in a casserole dish with crusty black edges.

"Shut up! Shut up! Heh, heh, heh!"

The large old oak dining table had carved lion's paw feet and freshly gnawed edges. "That danged bird has been chewing the furniture again," grumbled Aunt Fan, setting the casserole down beside a very large dish of pickles. "Come and get it, everybody."

"It smells interesting, Auntie," said Mrs. Rumpel, as they sat down at the table.

"It's a new recipe," said Aunt Fan. "I just invented it. Scalloped potatoes out of a box, combined with broccoli, zucchini and wieners. Very healthy."

"I can't stand scalloped potatoes," Leah whispered to her sister. "Or that other stuff. But I'm so hungry. What will I do?"

Quincy passed her the dish of pickles. "Eat the wieners and have some of these."

13
Susan Emma

When the casserole was replaced with a large bowl of tapioca pudding, Morris began to make peculiar sounds.

"What's the matter with him?" asked Aunt Fan, dishing up the pudding.

"Nothing. Absolutely nothing." Mrs. Rumpel glared at her youngest offspring.

"He's just gagging," said Leah.

"Fish eyes," spluttered Morris, staring at his serving. "It looks like fish eyes, or snake eggs, or—"

"So," said Quincy loudly, "when do we start looking for Grams?"

"We must start first thing in the morning," replied Aunt Fan.

"We just have to find her," said Leah, who was hungrily eating the creamy bits of her tapioca pudding. "We have to give Grams her birthday present tomorrow."

Aunt Fan nodded. "And the *next* day is the tournament. Grams would never miss that."

The Rumpels looked at her in surprise. "What tournament?"

"The big carpet bowling tournament at the retirement home. Grams is on the team. She's quite fond of sports, you know."

Kip looked up with interest. "Then I'll bet she'll be at the SkyDome tomorrow. The Jays are playing the Yankees and it's a big game. Maybe we should look for her there."

"Right on," cried Morris. "And afterwards we can go to the Hockey Hall of Fame."

"Maybe we should start with the revolving restaurant in the CN Tower," suggested Mr. Rumpel, nudging his pudding over towards his wife. "We might get a bite to eat while we're there."

Mrs. Rumpel wiped her chin daintily with her serviette. "Don't you think Grams would more likely go to the Eaton Centre? They say it's a spectacular marketplace of fashion and fun."

"Or she might be at the Science Centre," said Quincy, "exploring space."

Leah, who was still trying to fill up on pickles, mumbled only, "Niagara Falls."

***

That night, Mr. and Mrs. Rumpel bedded down in the guest room, Kip and Morris in the living room, and Leah and Quincy on a sofa bed in the den.

"I'm glad I'm not sleeping in the living room, with Prince Albert flopping around overhead all night," said Leah, who was sitting up in bed, brushing her hair.

"I think he goes in a cage at night," said Quincy, as she prowled around their small room. "I heard him sort of swearing at Aunt Fan when she put him in."

"He's so rude. I wonder why she keeps him?"

"I suppose because he was Great-granddad's. He's in that picture with him. They must have been very close." Pausing in front of a small oval mirror, Quincy scooped her hair up off her neck. Holding it in place on top of her head, she gazed intently at her reflection. "Do you think I look like that picture of Grams, when she was young?"

"You look more like Aunt Fan, now that she's got red hair, too."

Quincy frowned. "Leah, I don't consider that very complimentary. Aunt Fan must be at least fifty years old. Maybe even older."

Opening the sliding glass door of a bookcase, Quincy picked up some of the books. They were mostly old. There was a Bible of Aunt Fan's, an early edition of *Anne of Green Gables*, also with Aunt Fan's name in it. Then there was a well-worn book inscribed in faded purple ink:

Happy birthday to Susan Emma,
With love from Mother and Father.

Susan Emma . . . that's Gram's name. She must have loved this book. It's almost falling apart . . .

53

"Wow! Leah, look at this. It's *Around the World in Eighty Days*! And it used to be Grams'. I've never seen the book before — only the movie. Remember when we saw it on TV that time? Wow. Grams even marked some parts with red pencil. Just listen to this: *The project was a bold one, full of difficulty, perhaps impracticable.* Doesn't that just inspire you?"

There was no response. Leah had fallen asleep as soon as her head hit the pillow.

Taking the old book with her, Quincy climbed into the other side of the bed, burrowed down, and began to read.

14

Silly Us Frogs

"Avast, you lubbers! Hit the deck!"

Quincy woke up with a start. "Did somebody call me?"

Sitting on the bookcase, preening his feathers, was Prince Albert.

"Where did he come from?"

"I guess Aunt Fan let him out of his cage," said Leah, who was rummaging around in her suitcase. "I'm just so mad! I brought all the wrong clothes. I thought we were going to be at the cottage, not in the middle of the city. Which do you think I should wear today — my denim shorts, or my pink ones without pockets?"

"Leah, I don't care. Your denims, I guess."

"I think I'll wear my pink ones. You were talking in your sleep last night, you know."

"I was? What did I say?"

"Not much. It was pretty dumb. It sounded like 'silly us frogs.' You kept saying it over and over."

"Silly us frogs . . . silly us frogs . . ." Suddenly Quincy threw off the covers and sat bolt upright.

"It's from *Around the World in Eighty Days*. I was reading it last night. Leah, you've got to read it when you get older. It's pretty heavy stuff, but it's *really inspiring* . . ." Quincy stopped short.

"What's the matter?"

"That's it. I'll just bet that's it! Grams has been inspired to go around the world ever since she read this book when she was young, and *now she's doing it*."

"Quincy, she's ninety-one years old."

"That wouldn't stop me if I was ninety-one. And I'd love to do it in a hot air balloon, that's how. . . . Maybe that's what Grams did! I wonder if they have balloon excursion trips around the world . . ."

"It would cost an enormous lot of money."

"H'mmm. Well, maybe that's what she's been saving those moonstones for—to finance this trip."

Flushed with excitement, Quincy hopped about the room on one leg, yanking up her flowered overalls.

"Why, she might be floating somewhere over Manitoba by now. I've got to tell Aunt Fan . . ."

"Do you think Mr. Panagopolous went, too?"

"Sure. He would be like Passepartout, the valet. . . . Omigosh—both their names start with P!"

"Was he the hero?"

Mumbling something, Quincy bolted out of the room.

"What? I didn't hear you. Did you say *silly us frogs was*?"

"Phileas Fogg," Quincy called back. "Phileas Fogg was!"

In the kitchen, everyone was eating shredded wheat as Quincy and Leah burst in.

"I think I know where Grams has gone," announced Quincy breathlessly. "She's—"

"Gone around the world in a hot air balloon!" blurted out Leah. "Because Quincy said silly us frogs in her sleep. Well, not really said that, but that's what it sounded like . . ."

"What are you talking about?" cried Mrs. Rumpel.

"It wasn't silly us frogs," said Quincy. "I was saying *Phileas Fogg*. From that book of Grams' in the den— *Around the World in Eighty Days*."

Aunt Fan nodded. "That used to be Mother's favourite. And so . . . ?"

"And so maybe that's what Grams has done—gone around the world! Like Phileas Fogg did. Don't you see? It was probably something she always wanted to do, and now she has a chance, with Mr. Panagopolous — whose name begins with P, by the way, just like Passepartout. Just imagine, Grams would get to see all those romantic places that Great-granddad saw — moonlight on the Arabian Sea, and all that."

"Quincy, that's preposterous," said her father.

"I'm not so sure," said her mother. "She sometimes gets feelings in her bones. Don't you, Quincy?"

"Yes, and I think I've got some now."

"But in a hot air balloon?" scoffed Kip. "That's kind of dumb."

Quincy's blue eyes flashed dangerously. "How so, Mr. Pickles? What do you know about it?"

Leah gasped. "Quincy, you're being rotten to Kip."

"Well, he was rude."

"Rudeness is no excuse for rottenness," declared Aunt Fan. "Quincy's idea sounds farfetched, but it's not totally without merit."

Quincy grinned.

"On the other hand," Aunt Fan went on, "I tend to agree somewhat with Leah. Mother has always wanted to go to Niagara Falls again, ever since the queen went there."

Leah beamed.

"However," she continued, "seeing as we have two vehicles, we can split our forces and cover both bases. I will take Quincy to the balloon field and check it out, just in case. The rest of you can make your way to Niagara Falls, and we will all rendezvous there later today. Everyone take P.J.'s and toothbrushes, too. It never hurts to be prepared."

"Roger and out," said Mr. Rumpel. "Who's coming with us?"

Torn with indecision, Leah, Morris and Kip hesitated. Then, because none of them had seen a hot air balloon up close, and they were going to end up at Niagara Falls later anyway, they all opted to go with Aunt Fan and Quincy.

15
Big Barney

"We will rendezvous at 1600 hours in front of the Skylon Tower," said Aunt Fan, as everyone prepared for departure. "Now, synchronize your watches, everyone."

First to leave were Mr. and Mrs. Rumpel. Wearing their best jeans and equipped with compass, maps and a large tote-bag, they waved happily as they went out the door. "See you at Niagara Falls," they cried.

As Quincy, Leah, Morris and Kip straggled out of the apartment with their backpacks, Morris suddenly ducked back inside, his baggy cut-offs swirling about his legs.

"Now where has that boy gone?" asked Aunt Fan. Wearing a pith helmet, khaki knee-length shorts and a safari jacket, she clutched Prince Albert's cage in one hand and in the other, a large Eaton's shopping bag.

"He forgot his money belt," Leah told her.

"Come on, let's move it," croaked Prince Albert.

"Be quiet, you pesky parrot," ordered Aunt Fan.

In the underground garage, she marched over to an ancient green Landrover sporting a Canadian flag on the antenna, and a bumper sticker saying *Save the Spotted Owl.*

"Oooh, this is a high step," cooed Leah, as she went to climb in.

"You are kind of short," said Kip. "Here, I'll give you a boost." Grabbing her elbow, he heaved her up.

"I guess it's easy for you, you're so tall," gasped Leah, as she tumbled inelegantly into the car.

I don't believe this, thought Quincy. *She was actually batting her eyelashes at him . . . I think I'm going to be sick.*

Aunt Fan gunned the motor and they roared out of the garage with their flag flying.

As they rattled down the street, dodging the traffic, Quincy hung onto the seat for dear life. "You're a pretty skookum driver, Aunt Fan."

"This is a piece of cake. You should have seen me in the army." Aunt Fan pointed out the window. "There's the SkyDome, and over there is the CN Tower."

As they whizzed past, Quincy craned her neck trying to see the famous landmarks, but everything was a blur.

Soon they were on the outskirts of the city and bumping down a country road. Prince Albert huddled in the bottom of his cage and closed his eyes.

Eventually they came to a wooden sign.

"What did that say?" asked Aunt Fan, as they hurtled past.

"It said *Hot Air Balloon Rides This Way,*" yelled Quincy. "And it pointed down that other little road—"

"I knew it was around here someplace," said Aunt Fan, backing up in a swirl of dust.

At last they arrived at a small shed with a windsock on the roof.

"I don't see any balloons," grumbled Morris, gazing up into the sky.

"There's one." Kip pointed to the grass, where a bundle of brightly striped fabric lay beside a larger wicker basket.

And parked in front of the shed beside a dusty pickup was an old yellow convertible.

"The Mustang!" cried Kip.

"We've found Grams!" shouted Leah.

"Where's the party?" croaked Prince Albert, looking startled.

Quincy's mind was reeling. *We found Grams, and it's all because I read a book last night — or part of it. Maybe I could work for the police, finding lost people. All I'd have to do is read their favourite book . . .*

Aunt Fan marched up to the desk, where a rumpled-looking person in a leather jacket was reading a flying magazine. "We're looking for Mrs. Twistle and Mr. Panagopolous. I believe that's their car out in front."

"Ah, yes. The old Mustang with the expired licence plate. A little old lady with a big red purse, and an old gentleman with a cane? Yes, they were here."

"I knew it," cried Quincy. "So, where are they now? Newfoundland? Saskatchewan?"

"As far as I know, they're still at Lazy Acres Bed and Breakfast. It's about sixteen kilometres away, over

61

that hill . . ." The pilot jerked his thumb over his shoulder. "I took them there myself yesterday, in Big Barney."

"Big Barney?" Aunt Fan raised her eyebrows. "Please be more explicit, young man."

"Our numero uno balloono. The one lying outside on the grass."

I don't understand this, thought Quincy. *Why would they stay there if they're on their way around the world?* "Only sixteen K? Why did you leave them there?"

"Because they wanted to stay for the barn dance last night. They could have come back with us in the truck, but the old lady didn't want to. I only took them for a short flight, you understand, because the weather was due to close in."

"I wish you wouldn't call her the old lady," said Leah, frowning. "Her name is Mrs. Twistle."

"Oops. Sorry."

"Well," said Aunt Fan, "I guess we'd better get over to Lazy Acres and pick them up."

It was then that Quincy got her big idea. "It wasn't a feeling in my bones," she told the others afterwards. "It was more like a lightbulb in my head."

She turned to Aunt Fan. "Maybe we could go to Lazy Acres in Big Barney . . ."

"Oh, man! A balloon ride!" whooped Morris.

"Right on!" cried Kip.

"Far out," said Leah in a small voice.

"I'll check the wind," said the pilot, going outside. Licking his finger, he held it up in the air.

"The wind is about right," he announced. "Yep, I think we could get there, if we left right away."

"But I haven't agreed to this," said Aunt Fan. "For one thing it would be costly, and for another I won't have Mother riding back in that truck. I am going to drive to this Lazy Acres place and bring her back in a proper vehicle."

"But, Aunt Fan, we have money. Or at least, Morris does," pleaded Quincy, looking hard at her brother. "We could pay for our own balloon ride and meet you there."

In the end, Aunt Fan not only relented but paid the whole cost. Morris's money belt, it seemed, was only full of coupons.

16

Rumpels Aloft

After winding a white silk scarf around his neck and turning his peaked cap around backwards, the pilot led them out to the balloon.

Quincy, Kip, Leah and Morris scrambled into the basket. Then, while Aunt Fan and the pilot's partner watched, the burner was fired up. And the orange-and-green-striped balloon slowly filled with hot air and began to rise.

At first there was the noise of the burner. Then the pilot shut it down, and everything went quiet.

Oh, yes, thought Quincy, as they drifted silently over the treetops. *Yes, yes, yes!*

She squirmed around in her seat and looked down. Aunt Fan was standing by the hangar, waving. Quincy waved back, but her great-aunt was getting smaller and smaller. Finally she disappeared altogether.

"You didn't wave to Aunt Fan," she said to Leah, who was sitting with her eyes closed, clutching the padded suede edge of the basket. Leah shook her head.

"Are we landing now?" she asked. "I hear chickens."

"Ducks. A bunch of ducks just flew past. Why don't you open your eyes and look? Leah, this is the most wonderful experience of my entire life. I wouldn't be surprised if I choose hot air ballooning for a career."

Leah cautiously opened one eye. "How much farther is it?"

"Is there any food?" asked Morris. "I was just thinking about French onion soup, a double burger with fries, and a chocolate shake."

Nobody here appreciates this like I do, thought Quincy. *Look at Kip. He's more interested in that noisy burner than in the scenery. And all Morris thinks about is his stomach . . .*

Eventually Leah relaxed her grip on the edge and opened both eyes. She looked down and waved to some cows.

"Herb thinks we're going about five knots an hour right now," said Kip.

But even as he spoke, the wind changed. Suddenly it was coming from the opposite direction.

"We're turning around!" gasped Leah, grabbing Quincy's arm.

"We're going back to the hangar!" cried Morris. "Oh, boy, that was a short trip!"

As the balloon dipped in the freaky summer breeze, Quincy peered down, observing the countryside below. "There goes Aunt Fan in the Landrover . . . but it looks like she's going in the wrong direction!"

The pilot glanced down. "Yeah. She's headed back to Toronto. Now why would she do a dumb thing like that?"

"She hasn't got her glasses on," explained Leah. "She doesn't like wearing them."

As they floated closer, the three Rumpels and Kip could hear snatches of Aunt Fan singing cheerily. Then the breeze swooped them away.

After that they floated silently over the land, until the pilot pointed ahead to some farm buildings.

"Lazy Acres, coming up . . ."

"Here we come, Grams!" shouted Quincy.

"How are we going to get down?" wondered Leah.

"Um, well . . ." began Quincy. "I think there must be a rudder or something that you . . ."

"Piece of cake," said Kip. "Simplissimo. We release some of the hot air, and we float down."

"I knew that."

The pilot flung the end of his white scarf over his shoulder and adjusted his cap. Then he opened a valve at the top of the balloon. "Hang on, kids. Here we go!"

It's sort of like going down in a slow elevator, thought Quincy, as they sank towards the earth. As they skimmed the farmhouse, figures burst out the door, waving.

After landing between two haystacks, the pilot jumped out of the basket and tied the balloon down. Then he turned his cap around frontwards and put his scarf away in his pocket.

"Here comes Al to pick me up," he said, pointing to a cloud of dust barrelling across the field towards them.

"You mean you aren't going back in Big Barney?" asked Quincy.

"The wind would be all wrong. Balloons can't go against the wind, you know," said Kip.

"I knew that. I'd just forgotten. Come on, Leah, let's find Grams."

As she flounced off towards the farmhouse, she was trailed by Leah and overtaken by Morris.

"Somebody's making chocolate chip cookies — I can smell 'em!" he cried as he trotted off through the stubble, his nose twitching with anticipation.

17
Lelawalo

"*Welcome to Lazy Acres Bed and Breakfast,*" said the sign. "*Weekend Special for Seniors.*"

On the verandah, a little cluster of people stood watching curiously as the balloonists advanced towards them.

Quincy scanned the faces, searching for her great-grandmother. *Why, they all look the same,* she thought. *They all have white hair and glasses. And they're all wearing jogging shoes . . .*

"Grams . . . ?" she asked hopefully. "It's me, Quincy, from Cranberry Corners. Quincy Rumpel, that is. And these are Leah and Morris Rumpel, and Kip Twistle. We're your great-grandchildren."

But the people just stared solemnly back at her, the sun shining off their spectacles.

I don't think Grams is here at all! Oh, where is Aunt Fan when we need her . . .

Then a motherly lady in a checkered apron appeared from inside the house. "Little Mrs. Twistle with the pink velvet jogging suit and the big red purse? And

68

the old gentleman with the cane? Yes, they were here last night," she told Quincy. "I was a little worried that Mrs. Twistle might be overdoing it in the line dancing when she kicked her shoe off, but it didn't seem to bother her. They left early this morning, though. On the bus."

"Do you know where they were going?"

"They didn't say. But Mrs. Twistle mentioned a Lela somebody. Walo, I think it was. And there was something about horses. Now, why don't you young people join us for tea while you wait for your aunt?"

This the four balloonists readily agreed to.

As they followed the others into the house, Kip took off his cap and scratched his head. "*Lela Walo?* I wonder who that is? Probably some old friend of Gram's."

"I think it sounds like the name of a boat," said Leah, as they made a beeline for the table spread with little sandwiches, oatcakes, scones and chocolate chip cookies.

Lela Walo. The words ran around in Quincy's head as she munched a cucumber sandwich. *Somehow that sounds familiar . . .*

Then she exclaimed, "Boat — that's it! Lelawalo was the name of the Indian princess — the real Maid of the Mist! I read about it in one of the brochures. Grams *must* have gone to Niagara Falls after all!"

"I told you that a long time ago," Leah muttered.

"But what about the horses?" said Morris. "They could have gone to the horse races."

"More likely the RCMP Musical Ride. Sometimes that's on at Niagara Falls," Kip told him.

Just then the door of the farmhouse banged open and a familiar voice proclaimed, "Here we are at last. I don't know why they don't make those ridiculous road signs bigger so a person can read them. Where's Mother?"

It was Aunt Fan.

***

After a quick cup of tea and some scones, Aunt Fan was ready to hit the road again—this time for Niagara Falls.

"How come you always get to ride in the front?" grumbled Leah, as Quincy manoeuvred herself into the front passenger seat.

"Because maybe I have some things to talk to Aunt Fan about. Anyway, you get to sit beside Prince Albert."

"Well, lah-dee-dah."

"I'm going to have a melt-down," cackled Prince Albert, glaring at Leah.

"I guess Prince Albert's been in the family a long time, eh, Aunt Fan?" said Quincy.

"Not too long."

"But he's in that painting — the one you did of Great-grandpa in his admiral's uniform."

"I added the parrot for effect, like I did the uniform. I thought it made the picture more interesting."

"I do that lots of times with my paintings, too," said Leah. "Like, I added a ladybug to my dandelion picture, when there really wasn't a ladybug there."

"Well, lah-dee-dah," muttered Prince Albert.

"Oh, do shut up, you tiresome bird," said Aunt Fan. As she swung the car briskly onto the highway, everyone was relieved to see she was now wearing her glasses.

"Sometimes you don't seem to like him very much," said Quincy.

"Sometimes I don't. He's rude and he's mean."

"Then why did you get him?"

"Quincy, it's like they say about greatness. Some are born into it, some earn it, and some have it thrust upon them. One year at Lake Wannabanana I bought a whole book of raffle tickets on a lovely new powder-blue, 4-wheel-drive Jeep with disc brakes and all-weather tires . . ."

"They sure have good prizes at Lake Wannabanana," said Kip.

"Sometimes they do. I didn't win this one, though. But I did get third prize . . ."

"Twenty-five cans of purple paint?" suggested Leah.

"No, that was another time. This was— "

Somehow Quincy knew what was coming. "Prince Albert?"

Aunt Fan nodded. "Complete with his cage and a huge bag of sunflower seeds. He ate all the sunflower seeds the first day. And I haven't bought any raffle tickets since."

18
On to Niagara Falls

"So," said Quincy, as they clattered down the highway, "then our great-grandpa — your father — wasn't really an admiral at all?"

"Not really. He was a cook on a tramp steamer in the China Sea. I believe he made pancakes, mostly. Until they caught him smuggling."

Quincy gulped.

"Smuggling?" cried Kip, Leah and Morris from the back seat.

Aunt Fan nodded. "I'm afraid so. Moonstones. He brought home some beauties, too. But when Mother found out they were smuggled, she gave them all away to the Salvation Army."

"Oh, man!" moaned Morris. "She gave them away?"

"They were ill-gotten gains, Morris," said Aunt Fan. "Anyway, after that, Daddy left the sea and went looking for gold up north. We still didn't see too much of him, but he started to send home lots of money."

Morris fished a pencil and a wrinkled chocolate bar wrapper from his pocket. "Do you know where up north this place was?"

"I forget, and it doesn't matter, because he didn't find any gold. He did open a pancake restaurant, though, and that's what was successful."

"That must be why we all like pancakes so much," said Leah.

So that's the story of the moonstones, thought Quincy. *I guess it's no wonder Grams never talked about Great-grandpa. Still, I wish I'd known him . . .*

At last Morris spoke up. "My stomach's getting hungry for pancakes. Are we there yet?"

"Just about," Kip told him. "I think. Of course, I haven't been here for a while. Actually, it was the time one of the big hotels ran out of pickles. Dad and I had to make an emergency run out here to deliver ten cases of gherkins. It was pretty exciting."

"Ooh," squealed Leah. "You must have felt like a real hero, like you were rushing some kidneys or something to a hospital!"

Quincy groaned.

"It was pretty neat," admitted Kip.

Morris pressed his nose against the window. "I see lots of signs. There's one for a rollercoaster and, oh, boy, there's one for the Haunted House!" Opening his money belt, he took out his coupons and began checking them over.

"Listen, everybody. I think I hear Niagara Falls," cried Leah. "It's sort of a rumbling sound. Oh, this is *so* exciting. Just think, all that water has been pouring over those rocks for millions and millions of years, and millions and millions of people on their honeymoon have heard it, and now we're hearing it, too."

"We're not there yet," said Aunt Fan. "That's a double-decker bus you're hearing."

But they were getting close. And soon they did hear the unmistakable roar of the Falls themselves. "Over there," shouted Aunt Fan, stopping the car and pointing.

"Man!" cried Morris. "This is awesome!"

"I can't believe I'm here," yelled Leah. "Little old me, actually here at Niagara Falls!"

But as she gazed at the thundering water in all its tremendous power, Quincy was silent. *We're so small,* she thought. *We're all of us so small . . .*

Then she looked aghast at the heavy traffic and the teeming crowds. *Good grief. How will we ever find Grams in all this? Or even Mom and Dad . . .*

But she had reckoned without Aunt Fan. After squeezing her Landrover into a slot marked *Small Cars Only*, she managed to lead her troops, with only a few wrong turns, almost directly to the appointed meeting place — the prestigious Skylon Tower — right on the stroke of four.

And there, wonder of wonders, sitting on a bench outside sharing a bag of popcorn, were Mr. and Mrs. Rumpel.

"We just got here," said Mrs. Rumpel. "We got caught in the traffic."

"Well, at least we made it." Aunt Fan set down Prince Albert's cage. "Now to find Mother . . ."

74

"Popcorn! Popcorn!" screeched Prince Albert.

"When do we get to see the Haunted House?" whined Morris.

"Morris, just shut up about the Haunted House," said Quincy. "We're here to find Grams, remember?"

"And her birthday will soon be over and we haven't even given her our present yet," added Leah.

"Since she was talking about Lelawalo, the Maid of the Mist, we will start by looking there," decided Aunt Fan. "Mother always loved that boat."

"What about the Musical Ride?" asked Kip.

Aunt Fan looked thoughtful. "She does love horses, too, so we will look there also. And we should check all the hotels."

"Maybe we should check into one ourselves," said Mrs. Rumpel.

"Good idea!" Mr. Rumpel agreed. "While I'm checking the hotels for Grams, I'll find us some nice accommodation."

As he hustled away, Mrs. Rumpel called after him, "A view of the Falls would be nice . . ."

Mr. Rumpel turned and waved. "You betcha," he shouted. "This is a once-in-a-lifetime experience. Nothing will be too good for the Rumpels tonight!"

"Try and get heart-shaped beds," yelled Leah.

19

The *Maid of the Mist*

"Coming through ... coming through ... please make way, this is an emergency ..."

Lugging Prince Albert's cage and followed by Mrs. Rumpel, Quincy, Leah, Morris and Kip, Aunt Fan pushed her way through the throng of passengers waiting to board the *Maid of the Mist*.

"Have you seen a little old lady in a jogging suit and an old gentleman with a cane?" she asked the officer at the gangplank.

"Lady, I've seen lots of people like that."

"Pink," insisted Leah. "It's a pink jogging suit. And she had a red purse. It's our great-grandmother. She used to look something like me when she was young."

"You see," went on Quincy, "we have reason to believe she was coming here, because she was talking about Lelawalo. You know, the real Maid of the Mist."

"Shake a leg, you dirty landlubbers," croaked Prince Albert, glaring at the boarding passengers.

Mrs. Rumpel watched them enviously. "I've never been on the *Maid of the Mist*," she murmured.

"Oh, I'd love to go for a boat ride," said Leah. "Do you think we could?"

"It's a pretty rough ride," said Kip.

"And you'd have to wear one of those blue raincoats with a hood," Quincy told her. "And rubber boots."

"I wouldn't care."

"I think I smell hot dogs on that boat," said Morris, sniffing the air.

"That's the diesel engines," Kip told him. "Man, that's power."

"Aunt Fan," pleaded Quincy, "it wouldn't take very long for a little trip, would it?"

"Well, I suppose now that we're here . . ." Aunt Fan fished her wallet out of her pocket once again.

"Oh, a boat ride. Jolly good!" chortled Prince Albert. But as the search party donned their raingear and boarded the *Maid of the Mist*, Prince Albert found himself—due to ship's regulations—left behind.

"Dang-busted, horn-swaggled landlubber!" he muttered as a ship's officer lifted his cage to one side.

The boat pulled away from the dock, and Quincy worked her way to the bow. Her face dripping with spray, she peered into the mist as the little boat chugged closer and closer to the base of the Falls. Now the thundering roar was deafening. She could not see the top of the Falls — just the crashing waters and swirling mists.

I am Lelawalo, the beautiful daughter of the chief.

To save my people I will plunge over the Falls in my canoe . . .

Suddenly Quincy noticed the roar was subsiding. The boat had turned, and was heading back towards the landing. She looked around for the others, but everyone looked the same with their wet red faces and blue hoods. At last, as the crowd disembarked, she spotted Aunt Fan in her pith helmet striding down the gangplank, followed by Morris and Kip. Creeping along behind them, clutching each other, came two more figures — Mrs. Rumpel and Leah.

When they all reached solid ground, Aunt Fan said, "Now let's go and see if Mother is at the Musical Ride."

"I don't think I can," moaned Mrs. Rumpel. "My knees are all shaky."

"You'll feel better in a minute," said Aunt Fan. "A ride in the People Mover will do you good."

But when they got to the park, they found that the Mounted Police Musical Ride would not be on until the following week.

Quincy groaned. "Thirty-six horses. I would love to see them. Poor Grams. She must have been disappointed, too."

Suddenly Morris collapsed in a heap on the grass, clutching his stomach.

"Now what's the matter with him?" asked Aunt Fan.

"He's just hungry," said Leah.

"We're all hungry," said Aunt Fan. "Let's get on the People Mover and go back to town."

Back at the Skylon Tower there was still no sign of Mr. Rumpel.

"He'll probably get himself something to eat some-where," said Mrs. Rumpel. "We may as well go ahead without him."

"Burgers?" gasped Morris, as they roamed the streets looking for a restaurant. "Burgers, fries, shakes . . . ?"

But all such eating places were full. And so Aunt Fan, Mrs. Rumpel, Quincy, Leah, Morris and Kip eventually found themselves sitting on cushions on the floor of a Japanese restaurant, sipping green tea and waiting for their chicken teriyaki.

"Where are we going to look next?" wondered Mrs. Rumpel, who was feeling a little better after her tea.

"How about the Haunted House?" Morris looked up hopefully.

"Morris, I promise you, after we find Grams, you can go to the Haunted House. Tomorrow," said his mother. "We can all do some fun things tomorrow."

"I'd like to go on the merry-go-round," said Leah. "I just love merry-go-rounds, especially the white horses . . ."

"Horses!" cried Quincy. "Maybe that's it. Grams loved horses, so maybe that's where she is . . ."

Aunt Fan stared at her. "The merry-go-round?"

"Sure, why not? I love the merry-go-round. Leah loves the merry-go-round . . ."

"I do, too," admitted Mrs. Rumpel.

"See? It must be in the Twistle blood to love merry-go-rounds." Hurriedly downing the paper thin cucumber slice that had garnished her chicken, Quincy scrambled to her feet. "There must be one here, and I'm going to look for it."

"I'm coming with you," said Leah.

Kip stood up. "I know where it is. I'll take you there."

"If that's all we're getting to eat, I may as well come, too," said Morris, who had inhaled his dinner in two gulps.

"Go if you must," said Aunt Fan. "But I think you're wasting your time. Your mother and I will wait here and have some more tea until you get back."

As they went past the cloakroom, a pathetic voice called out, "Where's the party, mates?"

"Poor Prince Albert," murmured Leah. "He didn't get to go on the boat ride, and now he's stuck in there with all the coats. Maybe we should take him with us."

"Not on your life," said Quincy, Kip and Morris.

20

The Heart-shaped Bed

They had not gone far when they heard the haunting sound of a steam calliope.

"It's a merry-go-round," cried Quincy. "I'd know that music anywhere!"

As the prancing, gaily painted wooden horses with their wild manes and flowing tails whirled past, Quincy looked eagerly at the riders.

Kids. They're all kids. Aunt Fan was right. We're wasting time. She felt a crushing surge of disappointment.

Suddenly Leah cried out, "Quincy, look! In that swan sleigh — behind the white horse with the brown mane . . ."

As the swans flashed past, Quincy caught a glimpse of something pink sitting inside.

Then the music came to an end, and the merry-go-round slowed down.

Quincy hopped on and made her way to the swan. *Please let it be her,* she prayed. And then she saw the big red purse.

"Grams?" Quincy's voice was squeaky with excitement. "Is that you, Grams?"

The small white-haired person in the pink jogging suit looked up. "I'm a little bit dizzy, dear. Do I need another ticket to go around again?"

"Grams, it's me, Quincy Rumpel, from Cranberry Corners. I'm your great-granddaughter. And I think you should get off now. Here, let me help you . . ."

"Happy birthday, Grams!" cried Leah, Kip and Morris, as Quincy led the old lady off the merry-go-round.

Grams turned to Quincy. "Who are all these kids?"

"We're all your great-grandchildren. This one's Leah, and that one's Morris. We're Rumpels. And this tall one is Kip — he's a Twistle. And Aunt Fan and Mother are still at the Japanese restaurant. So somebody should go and tell them we found you."

"But I'm not lost," said Grams. "I just wanted to ride on the merry-go-round. I've always wanted a horse. But they wouldn't let me ride on these horses so I had to sit in that silly swan thing." She looked around vaguely. "Where's Mr. P.? I think he was sitting down somewhere . . ."

"I see him." Leah pointed to a nearby bench, where an old gentleman with a cane was dozing.

After dispatching Kip and Morris to fetch the others, Quincy and Leah led Grams over to the bench.

"So, Grams," said Quincy, sitting down beside her, "you've been really gallivanting around, I hear. Hot air balloon rides and everything. Wow!"

"Balloon ride? I think I went for a ride in one once. It was nice and smooth." Grams peered at Quincy. "What did you say your name was, dear?"

"Quincy, Grams. Grams, do you really want to go around the world?"

The old lady looked puzzled. "Do I have to?"

"No, no. Of course not. Grams, I was wondering why you don't live with Aunt Fan. She could look after you, make sure you don't get lost like this again and . . ."

"I told you, Quinty, I'm not lost," said Grams crossly. "And I don't want to live with Fanny. She's a terrible cook. She puts zucchini in everything — zucchini muffins, zucchini soup, zucchini sandwiches. And she's bossy, too. Then there's that awful bird of hers — some kind of canary, I think."

"It's a parrot, Grams." Quincy looked at the gentle, lined face of her great-grandmother. The blue eyes seemed clouded, and the silvery hair was thin and cut short, but she could still see traces of the laughing young girl in the photograph.

Maybe Grams used to look like Leah, she thought, *but I think she's really more like me. At least we like the same books, and she always wanted a horse, just like I did, before I got Roxy.*

Just then a familiar voice croaked, "Where's the party, mates?" Aunt Fan, Mr. and Mrs. Rumpel, Morris, Kip and Prince Albert were approaching.

After the hugs and kisses and shouts of "Happy birthday!" Grams was presented with the Polaroid picture of the Rumpels, now in a nice silver frame.

Quincy leaned over Grams' shoulder. "That's my horse, Roxy, sort of in front of Mom. If you come out to visit us, Grams, you can have a ride on her."

"And maybe I can paint your portrait," said Leah. "I'm going to take some lessons."

"You can sleep in my room," Morris told her. "With Leonardo and Donatello. They're pretty quiet, mostly."

Grams smiled happily. "This is a lovely birthday. How old did you say I was? A hundred?"

"You're ninety-one, Mother," said Aunt Fan.

"Where's my Mustang?" asked Mr. Panagopolous suddenly.

"It's at the balloon field," said Kip. "It's safe."

"Well," said Aunt Fan, "luckily everything has turned out all right, thanks to these young people. You had us very worried, Mother. I even put out a red button alert. But now I think we should go to our hotel. What did you find for us, Harvey?"

"I hope our rooms have a view of the Falls," said Mrs. Rumpel.

"Not exactly," said Mr. Rumpel. "It was hard to find any accommodations. But you're going to love our place. It's right close to a big Ferris wheel."

"Then let's get over there so Grams can have her birthday cake before she goes to bed." Aunt Fan picked up Prince Albert's cage.

"What kind of cake is it?" asked Grams.

"Chocolate zucchini mayonnaise. I made it myself."

Grams rolled her eyes. "I'm not in a hurry to go to bed, Fanny."

"What's the name of our hotel, Harvey?" asked Mrs. Rumpel.

"Well, it's not exactly a hotel. It's more of a bed and breakfast. I think it's called the Apple Blossom Inn, or some such."

Leah gasped. "But that's fab, Dad. I think that's the one with the heart-shaped beds!"

"Er, there's just one thing. They only had two rooms left, but they're big ones."

"That's all right," said Aunt Fan. "One for the boys and one for the girls."

"But what if there's only one heart-shaped bed in our room?" wailed Leah.

"Well," said her mother, "it's Gram's birthday. So if there is a heart-shaped bed, Grams will get it."

There was, and she did.

***

As Leah and Quincy lay in their rollaway beds listening to the distant roar of Niagara Falls and watching the coloured lights from the Ferris wheel sweep across the ceiling, Leah sighed.

"I never thought we'd actually get to ride on the *Maid of the Mist* with all those honeymooners, did you, Quince? It was *so* romantic."

Hoisting her pyjama-clad legs up in the air, Quincy began doing bicycle wheelies over her head.

"I didn't see that many honeymooners," she panted. "But I have to say, it certainly was a totally *myst*ifying experience!"

Collect the Quincy Rumpel Series!

Quincy Rumpel

Quincy Rumpel wants pierced ears, curly hair and a Save-the-Whales T-shirt.

Her sister, Leah, can't see why she shouldn't have pierced ears, too, while Morris, her brother, longs for a dog.

Mrs. Rumpel hopes for rain, so her job at the umbrella shop will thrive.

And the neighbours, the Murphys, just can't decide whether having the Rumpels next door is the best or the worst thing that ever happened to them.

ISBN 0-88899-036-7 $5.95   paperback

Starring Quincy Rumpel

About to enter grade seven, Quincy Rumpel is determined that this is the year she will make her mark on the world and become a star. As Mr. Rumpel tries to market his latest business venture, the Rumpel Rebounders, Quincy embarks on a grand plan to advertise the rebounders on television and ensure stardom for herself at the same time.

In this sequel to the enormously popular *Quincy Rumpel*, the whole eccentric clan is back in the rambling house at 57 Tulip Street — Leah, Morris, Mr. and Mrs. Rumpel, cousin Gwen and the Murphys. They are joined by crazy Auntie Fan Twistle and Quincy's latest heart-throb, Morris's soccer coach, Desmond.

ISBN 0-88899-196-7 $5.95   paperback

Quincy Rumpel, P.I.

Why is Quincy Rumpel creeping around the old Beanblossom house? Has she discovered the bizarre burial ground of the little dog, Nanki-poo? And what are the strange apparitions that her brother, Morris, sees in the house at night? How about the treasure that Captain Beanblossom left behind? And, most important, who else is interested in the abandoned house?

Quincy Rumpel is back again with an all-woman private investigating firm. But her best-laid plans soon go astray when she's joined by ever bothersome Morris, his best friend, Chucky, and her heart-throb, Freddie Twickenham, who is convinced that he has his grandfather's Mountie blood coursing through his veins.

ISBN 0-88899-081-2 $5.95   paperback

Morris Rumpel and the Wings of Icarus

Morris Rumpel, youngest member of the crazy and unpredictable Rumpel family, is on his way to the sleepy little town of Cranberry Corners to visit his grandparents for the summer. The trip brings surprises and adventures, from Morris's first airplane flight as an Unaccompanied Minor, to his attempts to learn to ride Fireweed (a horse with a mind of her own!), and a friendship with a family of peregrine falcons that lives near his grandparents' farm.

But the vacation turns out to hold more adventures than even Morris has bargained for. It begins the moment he is followed off the plane by a mysterious, icicle-eyed stranger, and the plot thickens as Morris gradually realizes that his new friends, the falcons, are in deadly danger . . .

ISBN 0-88899-099-5 $5.95   paperback

Quincy Rumpel and the Sasquatch of Phantom Cove

It all starts the day the Rumpels receive an invitation to visit their dear friends, Bert and Ernie, at their new fishing resort on the west coast. As Quincy and her family happily pack up the old stationwagon with beach gear, fishing poles and their trusty dog, Snowflake, they imagine lazy summer days spent lying on the dock, fishing and eating fresh salmon in the resort dining room.

But more than one mystery awaits them. The resort is a rundown dump, the Rumpels are the only guests, and there are no fish! When Quincy, Leah and Morris set out to discover why the fish have so mysteriously disappeared, they find signs of a very odd creature — a creature that looks a lot like a sasquatch!

ISBN 0-88899-129-0 $6.95   paperback

Quincy Rumpel and the Woolly Chaps

Quincy Rumpel — Ranch Nanny

This job title sounds great to Quincy Rumpel, who has just moved to Cranberry Corners with her family to help run her grandparents' ranch. She's desperate to buy a horse, and what could be difficult about taking care of a bunch of kids?

She soon discovers that the McAddams family is even crazier than the Rumpels — and even more prone to disaster.

ISBN 0-88899-160-6 $6.95   paperback